EPIC BOOKS are no ordinary books. They burst with intense action, high-speed heroics, and shadows of the unknown. Are you ready for an Epic adventure?

This edition first published in 2023 by Bellwether Media, Inc.

No part of this publication may be reproduced in whole or in part without written permission of the publisher. For information regarding permission, write to Bellwether Media, Inc., Attention: Permissions Department, 6012 Blue Circle Drive, Minnetonka, MN 55343.

Library of Congress Cataloging-in-Publication Data

LC record for Bugatti Chiron available at: https://lccn.loc.gov/2022020212

Text copyright © 2023 by Bellwether Media, Inc. EPIC and associated logos are trademarks and/or registered trademarks of Bellwether Media, Inc.

Editor: Kieran Downs   Designer: Jeffrey Kollock

Printed in the United States of America, North Mankato, MN

TABLE OF CONTENTS

A SHOW-STOPPING EXIT	4
ALL ABOUT THE CHIRON	6
PARTS OF THE CHIRON	12
THE CHIRON'S FUTURE	20
GLOSSARY	22
TO LEARN MORE	23
INDEX	24

A SHOW-STOPPING EXIT ≫

A crowd stares at a Bugatti Chiron. It is unlike any other car they have seen.

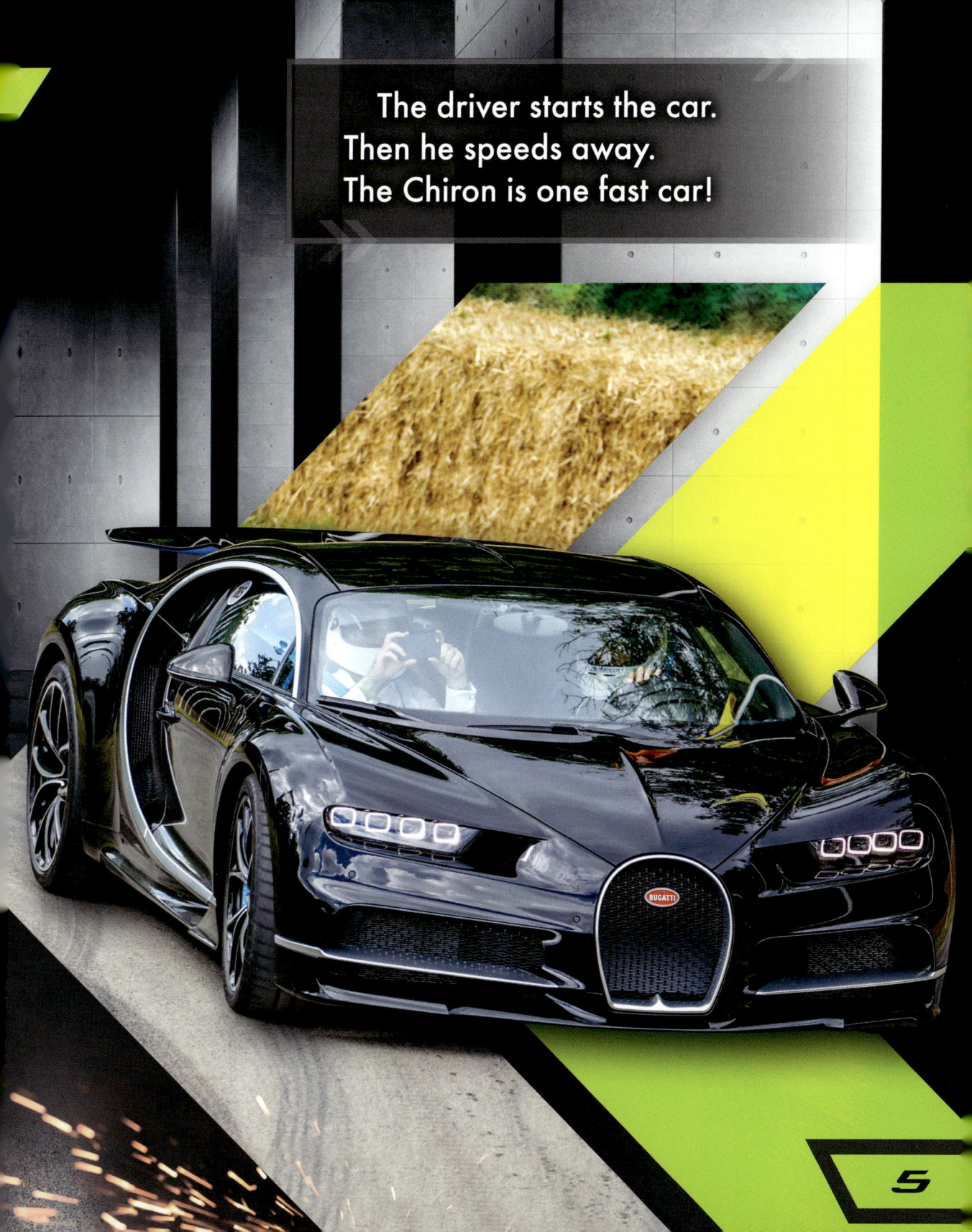

The driver starts the car. Then he speeds away. The Chiron is one fast car!

ALL ABOUT THE CHIRON >>

1930 MONACO GRAND PRIX

Bugatti began in Molsheim, France, in 1909. The company's early cars won many **Grand Prix** races.

Bugattis are known for their speed and eye-catching builds. Famous **models** include the Type 35, Divo, and Gran Turismo.

TYPE 35

📍 WHERE IS IT MADE?

EUROPE

MOLSHEIM, FRANCE

The Bugatti Chiron was first shown in 2016. Today, there are several Chiron models.

The Chiron is built out of lightweight materials. Its engine is an upgrade of the company's Veyron model.

2016 BUGATTI CHIRON

CHIRON BASICS

YEAR FIRST MADE — 2016

COST — starts at $3.3 million

HOW MANY MADE — 500

FEATURES

turbocharged W16 engine

horseshoe grille

C-shaped curves

The Chiron Super Sport is Bugatti's fastest car. It can reach speeds of 305 miles (491 kilometers) per hour. This is a world record for sports cars!

CHIRON SUPER SPORT

TRAINS AND PLANES
Bugatti has also made trains and racer airplanes!

Each Chiron is **custom-made**.
Owners pick their favorite colors and features.

PARTS OF THE CHIRON »

The Chiron has a large **W16 engine**. This helps it reach 60 miles (97 kilometers) per hour in 2.3 seconds!

Four **turbochargers** boost the engine. A seven-speed **automatic transmission** sends power to all four wheels.

ENGINE SPECS

QUAD-TURBOCHARGED W16 ENGINE »

TOP SPEED — 305 miles (491 kilometers) per hour

0-60 TIME — 2.3 seconds

HORSEPOWER — up to 1,578 hp

The Chiron has a lightweight **carbon fiber** body. A C-shaped curve runs along each side.

SPOILER

C-SHAPED CURVE

SIZE CHART

WIDTH — 80.2 inches (203.7 centimeters)

A horseshoe-shaped **grille** covers the car's front. **LED** taillights run across the back. A **spoiler** sits above them.

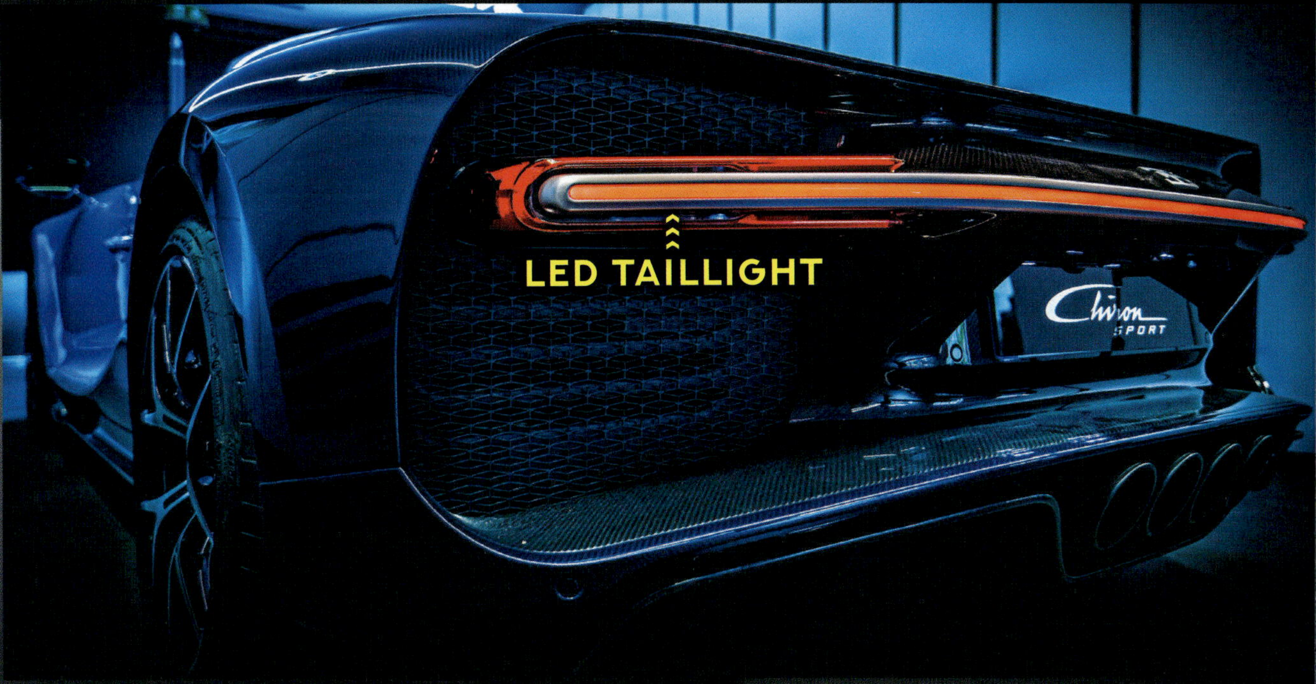

LED TAILLIGHT
Chiron
SPORT

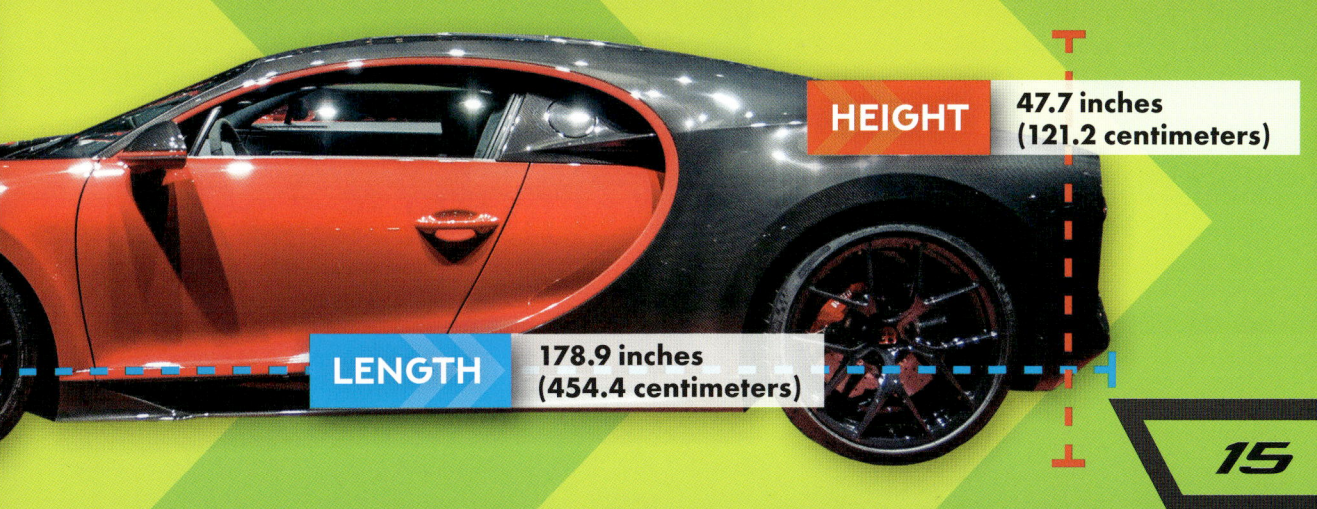

HEIGHT
47.7 inches
(121.2 centimeters)
LENGTH
178.9 inches
(454.4 centimeters)

The Chiron has a C-shaped **interior**. The inside can be built with a wide glass roof.

GLASS ROOF

INTERIOR

ALL IN A NAME
The Chiron is named after Louis Chiron. He won many Grand Prix races in a Bugatti!

Diamonds are included in the Chiron's speakers. A chilled glovebox can keep the driver's drinks cold.

CHIRON SPORT

The Chiron Sport and Pur Sport are popular models. They are built light for more speed.

These models have improved steering. They also have more powerful **suspension systems**. These give the cars extra smooth **handling**.

FAST BUT PRICEY

With great speed comes a higher price. The Pur Sport model costs $3.6 million!

CHIRON PUR SPORT

THE CHIRON'S FUTURE »

In 2021, Bugatti stopped making Chirons. The company was also bought by Rimac in 2021. Rimac is known for its **electric cars**. Bugatti Rimac will continue making some of the world's fastest cars!

RIMAC ELECTRIC CAR

A NEW PARTNERSHIP

Bugatti Rimac hopes to produce the first electric Bugatti by 2030.

GLOSSARY

automatic transmission—a car part that shifts gears for the driver

carbon fiber—a strong, lightweight material

custom-made—made to a particular customer's order

electric cars—cars that do not need gas to run

Grand Prix—a high-level racing competition

grille—a set of bars that cover an opening on the front of a car; the grille allows air to enter and exit the engine.

handling—how a car performs around turns

interior—the inside of a car

LED—a type of light that saves energy and takes a very long time to burn out

models—specific kinds of cars

spoiler—a part on the back of a car that helps the car grip the road

suspension systems—series of parts that help cars grip the road and move more smoothly over bumps

turbochargers—parts in an engine that increase horsepower

W16 engine—an engine with 16 cylinders arranged in the shape of a "W"; cylinders are parts in a car's engine that take gasoline and turn it into power.

TO LEARN MORE

AT THE LIBRARY

Durkin, Megan Ray. *Bugatti Veyron*. Minnetonka, Minn.: Kaleidoscope Publishing, 2019.

Hamilton, S.L. *World's Fastest Cars*. Minneapolis, Minn.: Abdo Publishing, 2020.

Smith, Ryan. *Bugatti*. New York, N.Y.: AV2, 2021.

ON THE WEB

Factsurfer.com gives you a safe, fun way to find more information.

1. Go to www.factsurfer.com.

2. Enter "Bugatti Chiron" into the search box and click 🔍.

3. Select your book cover to see a list of related content.

INDEX

automatic transmission, 12
basics, 9
body, 14
builds, 7, 8, 16, 18
Chiron, Louis, 17
colors, 11
company, 6, 10, 20, 21
electric cars, 20, 21
engine, 8, 12
engine specs, 12
glovebox, 17
Grand Prix, 6, 17
grille, 15
handling, 19
history, 6, 8, 20
interior, 16
materials, 8, 14, 16, 17
models, 7, 8, 18, 19
Molsheim, France, 6, 7
name, 17
price, 19
Pur Sport, 18, 19
racing, 6, 10, 17
Rimac, 20, 21
size chart, 14–15
speakers, 17
speed, 5, 7, 10, 12, 18, 19, 20
spoiler, 14, 15
Sport, 18, 19
Super Sport, 10
suspension systems, 19
taillights, 15
turbochargers, 12, 13

The images in this book are reproduced through the courtesy of: Unknown, front cover, p. 1; Tanase Sorin Photographer, p. 3; pbpgalleries/ Alamy, pp. 4, 5; Shawshots/ Alamy, p. 6; lorenzacciuss, p. 7; Dong liu, pp. 8-9; VanderWolf Images, p. 9 (isolated, grille); Heinz Reutersberg/ Wiki Commons, p. 9 (engine); Jack Skeens, p. 9 (curves); WEN Ltd, pp. 10-11; Grzegorz Czapski, pp. 11, 12 (engine), 14 (width); Wes Tindel/ Unsplash, pp. 12-13, 14; Matti Blume/ Wiki Commons, p. 13 (turbochargers); Fabe Collage/ Unsplash, p. 15; cristian ghisla, pp. 14-15 (length); classic topcar, pp. 16-17; Flavien/ Unsplash, p. 17; AaronTsui, p. 18; Ethan Yetman, pp. 18-19; Kaukola Photography, pp. 20-21 (rimac); Jarat Maletych, pp. 20-21.